Licensed exclusively to Top That Publishing Ltd
Tide Mill Way, Woodbridge, Suffolk, IP12 1AP, UK
www.topthatpublishing.com
Text copyright © 2015 Tide Mill Media
Illustrations copyright © 2015 Dubravka Kolanovic
All rights reserved
0 2 4 6 8 9 7 5 3 1
Manufactured in China

Written by Eilidh Rose
Illustrated by Dubravka Kolanovic

ISBN 978-1-78244-906-5

A catalogue record for this book is available from the British Library

Little Penguin

Written by Eilidh Rose

Illustrated by Dubravka Kolanovic

It was an
important day
for Little Penguin.

He was going swimming for the very first time!

Little Penguin was *nervous* about learning to swim ...

but he wanted to *splash* and play with his friends.

So he started to slowly waddle along the icy path towards the big, blue ocean.

Little Penguin was shuffling through the snow, practising **flapping** his flippers and **wiggling** his feet, when he saw Little Bird hopping towards him.

'I'm learning to fly!' said Little Bird.

'Are you Scared?'
asked Little Penguin.

'Not really. I'm not very good yet,
but I can almost get off the ground,'
said Little Bird, proudly.

Little Penguin continued down the icy path to the ocean. Suddenly, he saw a black shadow on the fluffy white snow.

High above him in
the bright blue sky
was Little Bird,

twirling

and SWOOping through the air.

'I'm finally flying!'
Little Bird squawked, happily.

As he was practising wiggling his feet, Little Penguin heard a splash and Little Seal jumped up on the ice beside him.

'I'm learning to fish!' said Little Seal, happily.

'Are you *nervous?*' asked Little Penguin.

'Not really. I haven't caught anything yet, but it's lots of fun!'

Little Seal saw a school of fish swimming past, so she plunged back into the water.

Waddling on, Little Penguin heard a big **splash** and an excited shout.

'Look, Little Penguin!'
cried Little Seal. 'I caught a fish!'
Little Seal **whizzed** off to show
all of her other friends.

Little Penguin felt tired
so he sat down for a rest.

As he was sitting on the ice,
a big wave splashed him.

'Sorry, Little Penguin,' said Little Whale.
'I'm learning to jump.'

'Are you **scared?**' asked Little Penguin.

'Not really. So far I've only done bellyflops, but I can almost get high enough for big jumps,' said Little Whale, weaving through the waves.

As Little Penguin got to his feet and shuffled on, he saw a shape jumping high above him.

It was Little Whale, leaping above the waves!

'Look at this one!' cried Little Whale, somersaulting through the air.

Little Penguin was still worrying about
how to flaP his flippers and wiggle his feet.

He could see all of his friends **splashing** and **sliding** into the water, playing lots of fun games.

Little Penguin **waddled** to the edge and looked down into the deep, dark water.

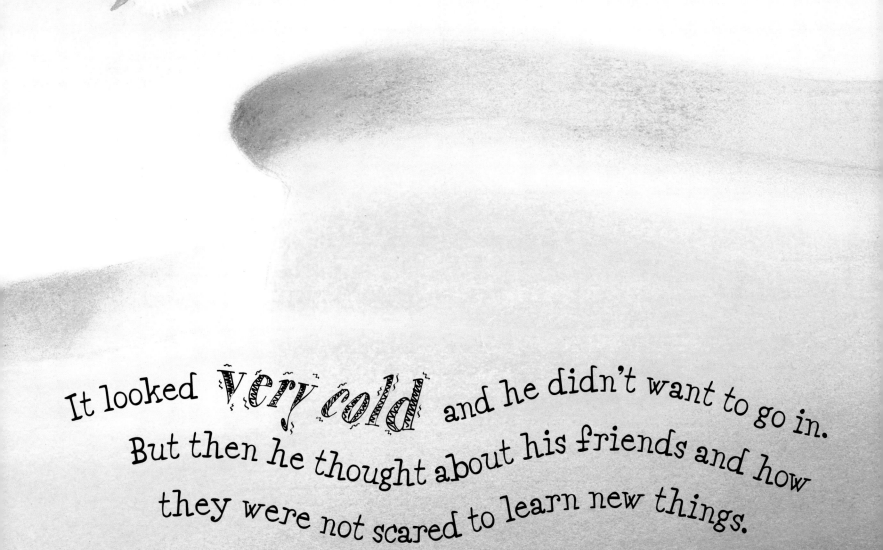

It looked **very cold** and he didn't want to go in. But then he thought about his friends and how they were not scared to learn new things.

Little Penguin shuffled closer
and, with a deep breath, slid on his
tummy and slipped easily into the water.

Just as he had practised, Little Penguin
flapped his flippers and wiggled his feet,

twirling and twisting through the water.

Little Penguin **whizzed** over to his friends to join in with their games.

Even though he had been nervous before,
Little Penguin could not wait to come
back for more fun tomorrow!